BROWN BABY Lullaby

Tameka Fryer Brown 🌙 ILLUSTRATED BY **AG Ford**

Farrar Straus Giroux • New York

For Niles, our three Brown babies, and brown babies everywhere. You are loved. —TFB

For my two sons—my little brown babies—Maddox and Carter. —AGF

Farrar Straus Giroux Books for Young Readers
An imprint of Macmillan Publishing Group, LLC
120 Broadway, New York, NY 10271

Text copyright © 2020 by Tameka Fryer Brown
Pictures copyright © 2020 by AG Ford
Printed in China by RR Donnelley Asia Printing Solutions Ltd.,
Dongguan City, Guangdong Province
Color separations by Bright Arts (H.K.) Ltd.
Designed by Monique Sterling
First edition, 2020

3 5 7 9 10 8 6 4 2

mackids.com

Library of Congress Cataloging-in-Publication Data

Names: Brown, Tameka Fryer, author. | Ford, AG, illustrator.
Title: Brown baby lullaby / Tameka Fryer Brown ; pictures by AG Ford.
Description: First edition. | New York : Farrar Straus Giroux, 2020. |
    Summary: An illustrated lullaby featuring a busy, independent, beloved
    brown baby being prepared for bedtime.
Identifiers: LCCN 2019004160 | ISBN 9780374307523 (hardcover)
Subjects: LCSH: Children's songs, English—United States—Texts. | Lullabies.
    | CYAC: Songs. | Lullabies.
Classification: LCC PZ8.3.B8157 Bro 2020 | DDC 782.42 [E] —dc23
LC record available at https://lccn.loc.gov/2019004160

Our books may be purchased in bulk for promotional, educational, or business use. Please
contact your local bookseller or the Macmillan Corporate and Premium Sales Department at
(800) 221-7945 ext. 5442 or by email at MacmillanSpecialMarkets@macmillan.com.

Look, mi hijo, at the sun
Setting now that day is done
Moonlight's breaking, night's begun

Come, my sweet brown baby

Zoom through every open door
Round the room and hit the floor

Bounce back up and zoom some more
Slow down, busy baby

¡Muy activo! In you go . . .
Hush now, here's your lovey–*oh!*
No, no, baby, we don't throw
No, no, antsy baby

Pots and pans all scattered round
Right-side up and upside down
Clanging, banging, noisy sound
Noisy, rowdy baby

Time to put the pots away
Bring them out some other day
Tired tears mean no more play
Vamos, fussy baby

Hands together as we bless
Food that *will* wind up a mess

That's okay . . . you're learning, yes?
Independent baby

Pour the cups and sink the sub
Grab a sponge to squeeze and rub
Keep some agua in the tub!
Silly, splashy baby

Yummy tummy, kissy cheeks
Tight black curls with glossy streaks
Clean and fresh and toddler-chic
One enchanting baby

Two brown eyes, one brown nose
Ten brown fingers, ten brown toes

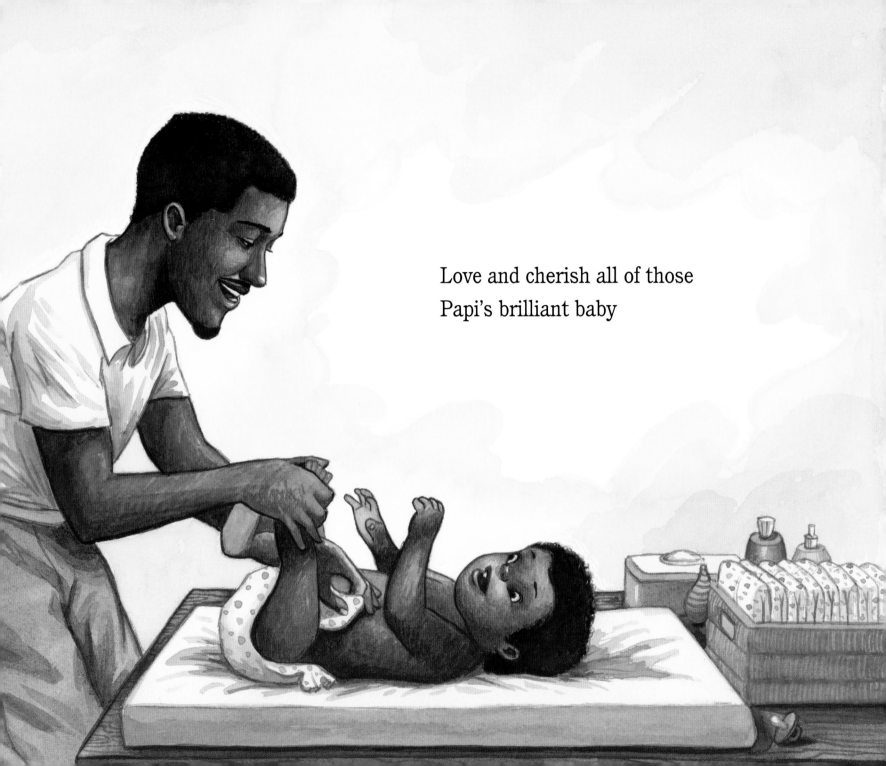

Love and cherish all of those
Papi's brilliant baby

Rub your eyes to Coltrane's song
Babble, clap, and stomp along
Fight that sandman till he's gone
Strong-willed, sleepy baby

Find your favorite book and then
Momma reads it once again

Lie you down and tuck you in
Buenas noches, baby

We love you . . .

Sweet brown baby